FULL COLOR
CAPTAIN UNDERPANTS
AND THE WRATH OF THE WICKED WEDGIE WOMAN

The Fifth Epic Novel by

DAV PILKEY

with color by Jose Garibaldi

Scholastic Inc.

Copyright © 2001 by Dav Pilkey
www.pilkey.com

All rights reserved.
Published by Scholastic Inc., Publishers since 1920.
SCHOLASTIC and associated logos are trademarks and/or
registered trademarks of Scholastic Inc. CAPTAIN UNDERPANTS,
TREE HOUSE COMIX, and related designs are trademarks
and/or registered trademarks of Dav Pilkey.

The quote by Albert Einstein is from an interview
in the October 26, 1929, issue of The Saturday Evening Post.

Library of Congress Control Number: 2017939694
ISBN 978-1-338-21623-3

18 17 16 15 14 13 12 11 10 9   20 21 22 23 24

Cover design by Dav Pilkey and Phil Falco
Book design by Dav Pilkey, Kathleen Westray, and Phil Falco
Color by Jose Garibaldi

Printed in China   62
First color edition printing, January 2018

"Imagination is more
important than knowledge."
—Albert Einstein

CHAPTERS

Hi everybody. Before you read this story, there's some stuff you need to know.

Read this comic book to fill yourself in on the story so far. But remember: This info is TOP-SECRET! So don't let it fall into the wrong hands!

The TRUBBLE WiTH CAPTAIN UNDeRPANTS

NOW it can BE TOLD !!!!!!!

--A inFORMashonal comic By George and Harold.

Onse upon a time There were Two cool Kids named George and Harold.

We KiCK Butt.

Me Too.

BuT They had a mean principLe named MR. Krupp.

Come over Here, Bubs!

NO WAY

One time George and Harold HipnoTized MR. KRupp with the 3-D HiPNO-RING™

You will OBey our comand.

O.K.

ZAP.

George and Harold made him think he was A GReaT super Hero Named Captain Underpants.

LooK--- I'm CAPTAIN UNDeRpaNTs!

HA HA HA

It was funny at first, But then mr. Krupp Jumped out the Window.

HEY WHERE do you Think YOUR Going?

To fight crime, ok?

George and Harold Had to chase After Him so he wouldént get killed and hurt.

Come over Here, Bub!

NO WAY!

They had many advenchures with Lots OF inapropreate HUMOR.

DIAPERS and TOILETS and poop... OH my!

PP

Then one day MR. Krupp Askidentelly drank super Juice.

super power Juice

GLUB GLUB

Now He gots super powers. He can FLY Too!

TRA-LA Laaaaa!!!

Two things you half to be careful About is: water and finger Snaps.

↓ H2O

↘ **SNAP**

FOR iF you SNAP YOUR Fingers by MR. KRUPP...

SNAP

...He Turns into Captain Underpants.

TRA-LA LAAAA!

And iF You PORE WATER on Captain Under- Pantses Head...

...He Turns BACK into MR. KRupp.

BLAH BLAH BLAH

So... IF you see MR. Krupp, don't Snap your fingers or YOU'LL BE SORRY.

And if you see CAPTain Underpants, don't pore no water on his head or youll BE SORRYER!!!

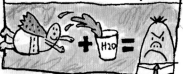

Remember- This is **TOP-SECRET** so don't tell Anybody!!!

Treehouse comix

I NC.

CHAPTER 1
GEORGE AND HAROLD

This is George Beard and Harold Hutchins. George is the kid on the left with the tie and the flat-top. Harold is the one on the right with the T-shirt and the bad haircut. Remember that now.

PEOPLE- PLEASE WEAR YOUR SOCKS ON THE GYM FLOOR

At most schools, the teachers try to emphasize "the three **R**s" (**R**eading, '**R**iting, and '**R**ithmetic). But George and Harold's teacher, Ms. Ribble, was more concerned with enforcing what she called "the three **S**s" (**S**it down, **S**hut your pie holes, and **S**TOP DRIVING ME CRAZY!).

While this was unfortunate for all of her students, it was especially bad for

George and Harold, because they were very imaginative boys.

You see, imagination was not really encouraged at George and Harold's school—in fact, it was discouraged. Imagination would only get you a one-way ticket to the principal's office.

This was sad for George and Harold, because they didn't get straight As, they weren't sports stars, and they could barely walk down the hallway without getting into trouble . . .

See what I mean?!!?

But George and Harold had one thing that most of the other folks at Jerome Horwitz Elementary School didn't have: *imagination*. They were *full* of it! And one day they would use that imagination to save the entire human race from being overthrown by a crazed woman with even crazier super powers.

But before I can tell you that story, I have to tell you *this* story . . .

14

CHAPTER 2
MS. RIBBLE'S BIG NEWS

One fine day, George and Harold's homeroom teacher, Ms. Ribble, entered the classroom looking a bit meaner than usual.

"Alright, settle down!" shouted Ms. Ribble. "I have some bad news: I'm retiring."

"Hooray!" cried the children.

"Not today!" snapped Ms. Ribble. "At the end of the school year!"

"Aww, *maaaan,*" moaned the children.

"But the staff is throwing a retirement party for me today . . ." said Ms. Ribble.

"Hooray!" cried the children.

". . . during recess," said Ms. Ribble.

"Aww, *maaaan,*" moaned the children.

"There will be lots of free ice cream!" said Ms. Ribble.

"Hooray!" cried the children.

"My favorite flavor: *chunky tofu!*" said Ms. Ribble.

"Aww, *maaaan*," moaned the children.

"But first," said Ms. Ribble, "it's time for something fun!"

"Hooray!" cried the children.

"You all get to make 'Happy Retirement' cards for me!" said Ms. Ribble.

"Aww, *maaaan*," moaned the children.

16

CHAPTER 3
WHEN YOU CARE ENOUGH TO SEND THE VERY BEST

Ms. Ribble went around the classroom handing out envelopes, sheets of construction paper, and butterfly stencils to all of the children. Then she wrote a poem on the chalkboard.

"Alright, take out your crayons," said Ms. Ribble harshly. "I want you to use stencils to make a yellow butterfly on the front of your cards. When you're done, copy this poem on the inside."

"Can we make up our own poems?" asked Melvin Sneedly.

"*No!*" snapped Ms. Ribble.

"Do we have to use stencils?" asked Aaron Mancini.

"YES!" yelled Ms. Ribble.

"Can we make our butterflies purple?" asked Stephanie Yarkoff.

"*NO!*" screamed Ms. Ribble. "Butterflies are yellow! Everyone knows that!"

While the rest of the class worked on their cards, George and Harold had a better idea.

"Let's make Ms. Ribble a comic book instead!" said George.

"Yeah!" said Harold. "We can make it all about her. It'll be cool!"

So that's just what they did.

CHAPTER 4
CAPTAIN UNDERPANTS AND THE WRATH OF THE WICKED WEDGIE WOMAN

By George Beard
And Harold Hutchins

CAPTAIN UNDERPANTS
AND the WRATH oF the
Wicked WEDGiE WoMAN

Story By George BEArd · Pictures By Harold Hutchins

Onse upon a time there was A really mean teacher named ms. Ribble who was very mean.

GRRRRR

I'm Am evil!

She gave us lots of homework and yelled at us all the time.

Read 250 Pages for A test!

AW MAN!

one Time at Chrismas Vacashion she gave everybody 41 Book Reports.

Ho Ho Ho!

Dec. 25

Wake up... It's time to open up your presints!

I cant! I half to do my homework!!!

After chrismas every-body turned in A Big Pile of book Reports.

HAW-HAW HAW!

Then something terible Happened.

CRASH

Help!

Ms. RIBBLE WAS BARied in A mounten of Book Reports

Shes REALLY Most SinSERLY Dead.

No Shes Not. We can Re-Build Her...

Docter

We can mAKe Her better than she WAS. ...Faster... Stronger... eviler!!!

Bionic LEG

Bionic LEG

operating table

surgen

Bionic Hair

Bionic ARM

Bionic ARM

When MS. RiBBLe got out of The hospiteL, She had Bionic Powers.

I wiLL Take over The World. HAW HAW HAW !!!

So she made a eviL Costume.

SNiP SNiP

Her Bionic Beehive Hairdoo opened up to Reveal a eviL wedgie ROBO-CLAW.

HAW HAW NoBody CAn stop me now!

inosent ByStander

OUCHies!

HeLP! wedgie Woman is in The teachers Lounge. She just drank all The coffEE and now shes giving the gym teacher A Killer-weDgie!!!

OH, The HORROR!! She better make A Fresh pot!!!

Principel

This LOOKS LiKE A **JOB** FOR...

CAPTAiN UnDERP. ANTS!!

CRASH

What'S the Problem, bub?

HeLp it's wedgie womAn!

Principel

So CAPtain Under- Pants got into A Big Fight with Wedgie woman. She tRied to give him A wedgie But...

Captain UnderPants was Faster than a speeding waistband...

ziP

... MoRe poWER- FuL Than Boxer Shorts...

OUCH

Pow

And abel to Leap tall bildings without getting A wedgie.

TRA-LA LAAAAA!

RATS

So Wedgie Woman went to the store to buy some spray starch.

NEW SPRAY STARCH

STARCH is The Enemy of underwear!

WARNING: DO NOT spray this product on your underwear OR youll Be sorry!

Wedgie Woman sprayed.

Gotcha!

HEY!

SSSSS

OH NO! My underpants is ALL stiff and uncomfertable!

HAW HAW

Captain underpants tried to push the buttons on his utility WAistband But they were broke!! HE WAS POWERLESS!

I'm DOOMED!

Wedgie Woman gave Captain Underpants A BIG Wedgie...

...Then she hung him from A pole.

RATS

NOBODY Can STOP me now!

Soon Some kids came by.

Captain Underpants needs our help!!!

So They Threw him a rope.

Catch!

Then they Pulled real hard.

And Let go.

Boing

SPLASH

Swiming Pool

The Kids PORed FABRIC softener in the pool.

FABRIC softener

Swim

sudenly the starch got washed away. HOORAY!!!

my underpants is soft and cottony onse Again!!!

HALLY-LOOYA!!

Swiming

thanks Kids

No problemo.

Soon captain Underpants Found wedgie woman.

Remember me?

Get Him ROBO-CLAW

He FLEW up...

It's we-dgie time!

... And Looped Around.

The ROBO-CLAW REACHED FOR Underwear...

... But it grabbed the wrong pair.

owie wowie

ITS OFF To JaiL WiTH YOU!

Aw MAn!

TRA-LA LAAAAA!

HOORAY!

THE END

NOTiSE: Any SiMALARitieS to actual persons (living or dead) is very, very unforchenate.

TReeHouse Comix INC.

CHAPTER 5
THE WRATH OF MS. RIBBLE

When Ms. Ribble read the comic book that George and Harold had made, she was furious.

"Boys!" she yelled. "You've just earned yourselves a one-way ticket to the principal's office!"

"But all we did was use our imaginations!" said George.

"You're not allowed to do that in this school!" snapped Ms. Ribble. "Didn't you read chapter 1?"

George and Harold gathered their things, and soon they were sitting in the office outside Mr. Krupp's door.

"Mr. Krupp is on the phone," said the school secretary, Miss Anthrope. "Why don't you boys make yourselves useful and copy the 'Friday Memo' for me! You can pass them out to all the classrooms for me while I go to lunch."

"Aww, *maaaan*!" said George.

"Quit your whining, buster!" shouted Miss Anthrope. "I want this done by the time I get back, or you'll *both* be sorry!" Miss Anthrope grabbed her coat and stomped out the door.

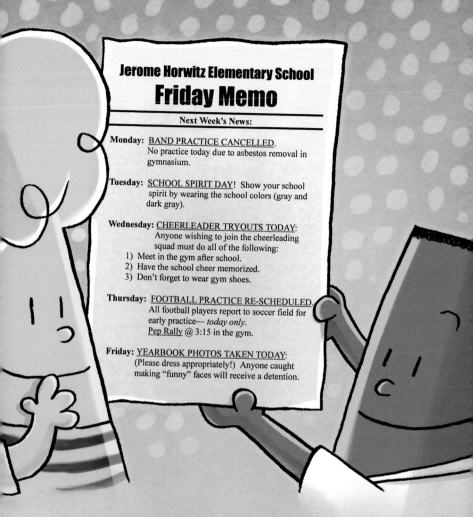

Jerome Horwitz Elementary School
Friday Memo

Next Week's News:

Monday: <u>BAND PRACTICE CANCELLED</u>.
No practice today due to asbestos removal in gymnasium.

Tuesday: <u>SCHOOL SPIRIT DAY</u>! Show your school spirit by wearing the school colors (gray and dark gray).

Wednesday: <u>CHEERLEADER TRYOUTS TODAY</u>:
Anyone wishing to join the cheerleading squad must do all of the following:
1) Meet in the gym after school.
2) Have the school cheer memorized.
3) Don't forget to wear gym shoes.

Thursday: <u>FOOTBALL PRACTICE RE-SCHEDULED</u>.
All football players report to soccer field for early practice— *today only*.
<u>Pep Rally</u> @ 3:15 in the gym.

Friday: <u>YEARBOOK PHOTOS TAKEN TODAY</u>:
(Please dress appropriately!) Anyone caught making "funny" faces will receive a detention.

George and Harold looked at the "Friday Memo." It was a weekly newsletter that told all about the events of the upcoming week.

"Hey," said George. "Miss Anthrope's computer is still on. Y'wanna make a few changes to this newsletter?"

"Why not?" said Harold.

33

Friday Memo

Next Week's News:

Monday: <u>SCHOOL CANCELLED</u>.
No classes today due to lack of interest.

Tuesday: <u>NATIONAL WEAR YOUR PAJAMAS TO
SCHOOL AND PICK YOUR NOSE DAY</u>!
Show you care by wearing your pajamas to
school (and picking your nose).

Wednesday: <u>CHEERLEADER TRYOUTS TODAY</u>:
Anyone wishing to join the cheerleading
squad must do all of the following:
1) Eat ten whole cloves of raw garlic
2) Draw a mustache on your face with permanent markers.
3) Tape a three-day-old egg-salad sandwich to your head.

Thursday: <u>FOOTBALL PRACTICE RE-SCHEDULED</u>.
All football players report to teachers' lounge
for early practice.
<u>Food Fight</u> @ 12:15 in the lunchroom.

Friday: <u>YEARBOOK PHOTOS TAKEN TODAY</u>:
(Please wear Bumblebee costumes).
Also, whoever makes the funniest face wins
a free pizza party for their class.

So George and Harold typed up their own
version of the Jerome Horwitz Elementary
School "Friday Memo." Then they ran off
copies for all the students in the school.

34

CHAPTER 6
THE RETIREMENT CARD

George and Harold were gathering their new-and-improved "Friday Memo" copies into small piles when Principal Krupp came into the office.

"Hey!" Mr. Krupp shouted. "What are you two troublemakers doing in here?"

"Miss Anthrope told us to pass the 'Friday Memo' out to all the classrooms," said George innocently.

"Well, make it snappy!" yelled Principal Krupp.

Suddenly, Harold got a sneaky idea. He took out the blank piece of construction paper that Ms. Ribble had given him earlier.

"Hey, Mr. Krupp," said Harold, "will you sign this retirement card for our teacher?"

Mr. Krupp grabbed the card from Harold and eyed it suspiciously.

"This card is *blank*!" Mr. Krupp growled.

"I know," said Harold. "Our class is going to decorate it later. We wanted you to be the first to sign it."

"Well, alright then," said Mr. Krupp.
He opened the card and quickly scribbled

Signed, Mr. Krupp

on the inside. Then he stormed out of
the office.

★ MINDLESS ★ CONFORMITY
IT'S COOL... IT'S FUN

BE JUST LIKE EVERYBODY ELSE!

INDIVIDUALITY CAUSES PAIN!

"What are you gonna do with that?" asked George.

"You'll see," said Harold, smiling.

38

CHAPTER 7
REVERSE PSYCHOLOGY

George and Harold passed out the "Friday Memo" and made it back to their classroom just in time for Ms. Ribble's retirement party. George quickly changed the letters around on the sign outside the door, while Harold wrote a special greeting on Mr. Krupp's card and stuffed it into the envelope.

"*HEY, BUBS!*" shouted Mr. Krupp as he stormed down the hall. "What do you kids think you're doing?"

"We're going to Ms. Ribble's retirement party," said George.

"That's what *YOU* think, smart guy!" said Mr. Krupp. "Ms. Ribble showed me that comic book you boys made about her. And now I catch you changing the letters around on another sign! You boys aren't going to any party . . . you're going STRAIGHT to the detention room!"

40

"Well *fine*," said Harold. "Then we're not gonna give Ms. Ribble the card our class made for her!"

Mr. Krupp quickly swiped the card out of Harold's hand.

"A-HA!" he shouted. "I'm going to make SURE she gets this card! I'm going to give it to her *MYSELF*!"

"Aww, *maaaan*!" said Harold.

SWIPE

MS. RIBBLE
REALLY NEEDS
A BREATH
MINT

George and Harold walked down the hallway toward the detention room.

"Wow," said George. "That was pretty cool how you got Mr. Krupp to deliver that phony card for you."

"Yep," said Harold. "I used *reverse psychology* on him!"

"I've gotta try that sometime," said George. "By the way, what did you write on that card?"

"You'll see," said Harold, smiling.

42

CHAPTER 8
THE PARTY

Ms. Ribble's retirement party started off bad, and just got worse. First, Ms. Ribble forced the class to sing a corny song to her. By the time she was done yelling at the boys for singing off-key, the chunky tofu ice cream was melted.

Everybody had to eat it anyway.

We Love Ms. Ribble
Written and Arranged
by Tara Ribble
"We Love Ms. Ribble
Oh Yes We Do.
We Don't Love Anyone
As Much As You.
When You Retire,
We'll Be Blue.
Oh, Ms. Ribble,
—We Love You!"

Then the children handed in their "Happy Retirement" cards. Ms. Ribble ripped several of the cards up because some of the children had mistakenly drawn polka-dots on their butterflies. One unfortunate boy had also drawn a happy smiling sunshine on his card, and he had to stand in the corner.

Finally, Mr. Krupp stepped forward and handed Ms. Ribble the card he had snatched from Harold's hand.

"I went to a lot of trouble to get this for you," Mr. Krupp said gallantly.

Ms. Ribble tore the envelope open and read the card out loud:

"You're One *Hot Mama*!" said Ms. Ribble, with a shocked look on her face.

"Eeeeeeeeew!" cried the children.

WILL YOU MARRY ME? Signed, Mr. Krupp

She opened the card and read the inside.
"Will you marry me? Signed, Mr. Krupp."
"Eeeeeeeeeeeeeeeeeeeeeeeeeeeewww!"
cried the children. The teachers gasped.
Then the room grew silent. Ms. Ribble glared
over at Mr. Krupp, who had turned bright
red and began sweating profusely.

He tried to speak. He tried to tell her
it was all a big mistake. He tried to say
SOMETHING . . . but all that came out was
"B-B-Bubba bobba hob-hobba-hobba wah-wah."

46

"Er, ummm, *congratulations*," said Mr. Meaner, as he patted Mr. Krupp's sweaty, shivering shoulder.

"Yes! CONGRATULATIONS!" shouted Miss Anthrope. "This will be the best wedding in the whole world! We can have it here at the school . . . a week from Saturday! I'll plan everything! You lovebirds don't have to worry about a thing!"

"Er-uh . . . great . . . thanks," said Ms. Ribble, still looking quite angry and confused.

"B-B-Bubba bobba hob-hobba-hobba wah-wah," said Mr. Krupp.

48

CHAPTER 9
FREAKY WEEKY

The following week at Jerome Horwitz Elementary School was definitely one of the weirdest ones they'd had in a while. For example: None of the kids showed up for school on Monday. But Mr. Krupp didn't even seem to notice.

"Hey, where is everybody today?" asked Mr. Rected.

"B-B-Bubba bobba hob-hobba-hobba wah-wah," said Mr. Krupp.

On Tuesday everybody did show up . . . in their pajamas!

"Why is everybody picking their noses?" asked Miss Fitt.

"B-B-Bubba bobba hob-hobba-hobba wah-wah," said Mr. Krupp.

On Wednesday, for some strange reason, the whole school smelled like garlic and rotten egg-salad sandwiches (especially some of the girls).

"Boy," said Ms. Guided, "the styles today sure are getting bizarre."

"B-B-Bubba bobba hob-hobba-hobba wah-wah," said Mr. Krupp.

51

Thursday was, without a doubt, a complete and total disaster.

"There's a food fight in the lunchroom!" shouted Mr. Rustworthy. "And the football team is destroying the teachers' lounge!"

"B-B-Bubba bobba hob-hobba-hobba wah-wah," said Mr. Krupp.

Now, *nobody* was sure what happened on Friday. Apparently, there was a mix-up with the dress code and the yearbook photos.

"Our school pictures are ruined!" shouted Ms. Dayken.

"B-B-Bubba bobba hob-hobba-hobba wah-wah," said Mr. Krupp.

Yes, it was a freaky week, alright. But the big wedding was only a day away . . . and things were about to get REALLY freaky!

53

CHAPTER 10
THE BIG WEDDING

It was Saturday, the day of the big wedding. Miss Anthrope, true to her word, had taken care of everything. In just one week, she had transformed the gymnasium into a beautiful wedding hall, complete with food, decorations, and even a six-foot-tall ice sculpture.

All of the children were dressed in their finest clothes. (Harold even wore a tie!)

"Man," said George, "I can't believe we have to go to school on *SATURDAY*!"

"I know," said Harold. "Why couldn't they have had this wedding during Monday's math test?"

Soon the organist began to play. The rabbi walked down the aisle. He approached George and Harold and stopped to talk to the boys.

"I've heard a lot about you two," said the rabbi, "and I don't want you boys playing any of your tricks today."

"Silly Rabbi," said George, "tricks are for kids!"

Believe it or not, George and Harold had not planned any pranks for the big wedding. They had no Joy Buzzers up their sleeves . . . no squirting flowers in their lapels . . . and no whoopee cushions on their chairs. They were on their best behavior. Nothing could go wrong today!

In no time at all, Ms. Ribble and Mr. Krupp were standing in front of the rabbi, looking quite ill. The rabbi asked Mr. Krupp if he would take Ms. Ribble to be his lawfully wedded wife.

"B-B-Bubba bobba hob-hobba-hobba wah-wah," said Mr. Krupp.

Then the rabbi asked Ms. Ribble if she would take Mr. Krupp to be her husband.

There was a long silence. Everyone leaned forward. Ms. Ribble looked nervously from side to side.

Suddenly, she shouted out at the top of her lungs, *"NOOOOOOOOOOOOOOOOO!"*

Ms. Ribble turned to Mr. Krupp and jabbed her finger into his shoulder. "Listen, Krupp," she said. "I *can't* marry you."

"Hooray! —er, I mean —*aww, that's too bad*!" said Mr. Krupp.

"You're a mean, cruel, and vicious man," said Ms. Ribble, "and I respect that. It's just . . . it's just . . ."

"Just what?" asked Mr. Krupp.

57

"It's just your *nose*!" said Ms. Ribble. "You've got the most *ridiculous* nose — I've never seen anything quite like it! I just couldn't marry somebody with such a silly nose."

Mr. Krupp got angry. "Well *fine*!" he shouted. "I didn't want to marry you anyway! It was all George and Harold's fault. They *tricked* us!"

Suddenly, everybody in the gymnasium turned and looked at George and Harold.

"Time to go," said George.

CHAPTER 11
THE REFRESHMENTS

As George and Harold turned to leave the gymnasium, they heard the loud thumps of cleated wedding boots clomping down the aisle toward them.

"I'M GONNA GRIND THOSE KIDS INTO HEADCHEESE!" screamed Ms. Ribble as she lunged for the two boys.

61

George and Harold screamed and ran to the back of the room near the refreshments. There they hid behind two large wooden pillars.

Ms. Ribble approached the pillars and grasped them with her mighty hands. With a horrible roar, she pushed the right pillar over. It landed on the back of the luncheon table, causing the front of the table to flip high into the air. Unfortunately, this sent all of the food flying into the crowd.

CRASH

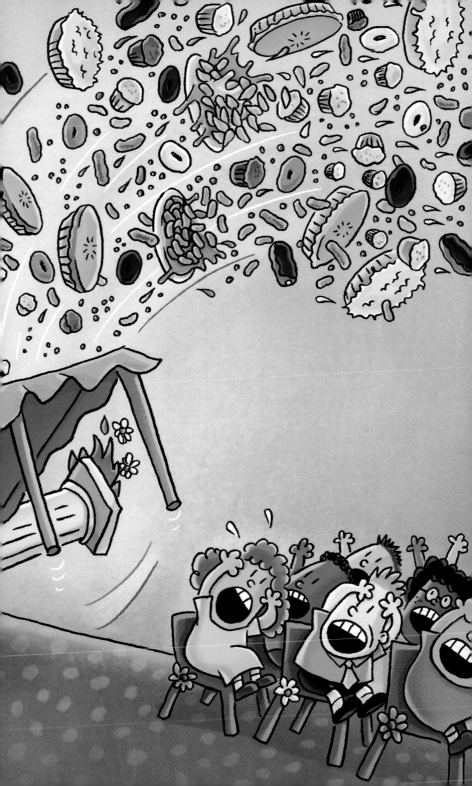

The creamy candied carrots clobbered the kindergartners. The fatty fried fish fritters flipped onto the first graders. The sweet-n-sour spaghetti squash splattered the second graders.

64

Three thousand thawing thimbleberries thudded the third graders. Five hundred frosted fudgy fruitcakes flogged the fourth graders. And fifty-five fistfuls of fancy french-fried frankfurters flattened the fifth graders.

65

By now you're probably worried that the
wedding guests had nothing to drink with
their lovely appetizers. Well, rest assured,
the second pillar took care of that. Ms. Ribble
pushed the left pillar into the fresh fruit
display, causing it to topple over, sending

66

two large watermelons crashing down into two oversized punch bowls. This created two enormous splashes of tropical fruit-flavored punch, which rained down upon the wedding guests like a torrential downpour.

67

Now, no wedding is complete without a wedding cake. And when Ms. Ribble kicked the ice sculpture over, the resulting crash sent the beautiful double-deckered cake flipping high into the air, right over Ms. Ribble's head.

68

"I'VE GOT YOU NOW!" screamed Ms. Ribble, as she grabbed George and Harold by their neckties.

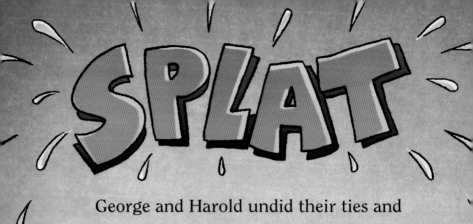

SPLAT

George and Harold undid their ties and ran out of the gymnasium screaming.

"Man," cried Harold. "I thought we were dead meat!"

"That's what we get for going to school on Saturday!" said George.

CHAPTER 12
RIBBLE'S REVENGE

As you might imagine, George and Harold were nervous about going back to class on Monday. But for some strange reason, Ms. Ribble seemed happy to see them.

"Good morning, boys," Ms. Ribble chirped with a giant, evil, toothy grin. "Come here . . . I've got something to show you!"

"Uh-oh," said George. "She's smiling—that *can't* be a good sign!"

George and Harold cautiously approached Ms. Ribble's desk.

"I took the liberty of adjusting your grades last weekend," said Ms. Ribble. "You'll be happy to know that all your grades have just dropped from Bs and Cs to *Fs* and *Gs*."

"Oh, *NO!*" George gasped. "Not *Fs* and *Gs*! Hey, what's a *G*?"

"It's the only grade *lower* than an *F*!" said Ms. Ribble.

"There's no such grade as a *G*," said Harold.

"There is now, bub!" said Ms. Ribble. "Looks like you're both going to *FLUNK* the FOURTH GRADE!!! Won't that be fun?"

"No way," said George. *"That's not fair!"*

"Life ain't fair," said Ms. Ribble. "Get used to it!"

CHAPTER 13
A BAD IDEA

That afternoon, George and Harold sat in their tree house feeling sorry for themselves.

"She can't get away with that," said George. "We've got to tell somebody about this."

"Nobody's going to believe us," said Harold.

"Well, there is *one* thing we can do," said George. He opened the drawer to their drawing table and searched through the pennies, paper clips, dried spitballs, and rubber bands. Then he pulled out a dusty plastic ring with some gum stuck on it. It was the 3-D Hypno-Ring.

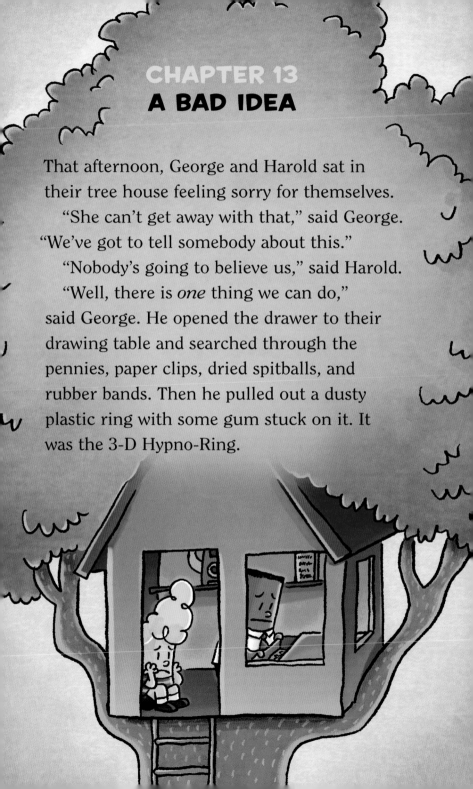

"Oh, no!" said Harold. "I thought we threw that thing away!"

"We just threw the instructions away," said George. "But I remember how it works."

"Do you *remember* what happened the LAST TIME WE USED IT?" asked Harold.

"Yeah," said George. "But we were fooling around last time. This time we'll be serious. We won't make any mistakes! All we have to do is hypnotize her into changing our grades back to normal. That's all!"

"I don't know . . ." said Harold. "It sounds like a bad idea to me!"

"Worse than *FLUNKING* the fourth grade?" asked George.

"Good point," said Harold.

74

CHAPTER 14
THE RETURN OF THE 3-D HYPNO-RING

The next day at school, George and Harold stayed behind while the rest of the class went outside for recess.

"What are you punks still doing here?" asked Ms. Ribble.

"Ummmm," said George nervously. "Er, we wanted to show you this really cool ring."

"Yeah," said Harold. "If you look closely at it, you can see a funny picture."

"Well, hold it still," said Ms. Ribble, as she stared at the ring intently.

"I have to move it back and forth," said George, "or you won't be able to see the picture."

Ms. Ribble's eyes followed the ring back and forth . . . back and forth . . . back and forth . . . back and forth . . .

"You are getting sleepy," said George.

"Veeery sleepy," said Harold.

Ms. Ribble yawned. Her eyes began to droop.

"I'mmssooosleeeeepyyy," she said, as she slowly closed her eyes.

"In a moment," said George, "I will snap my fingers. Then you will be hypnotized."

"Ssssssoooosssslllleeeeeeeeepyyyyyyy," mumbled Ms. Ribble.

SNAP!

"Now," said Harold, "you must listen very . . ."

CHAPTER 14 1/2
WE INTERRUPT THIS CHAPTER TO BRING YOU THIS IMPORTANT MESSAGE:

"Hello, this is Chim-Chim Diaperbrains . . . er, I mean, this is Ingrid Ashley reporting for Eyewitness News. We have a late-breaking story about a tragic incident that is now occurring in the Pacific Northwest.

"Police have just closed down the Li'l Wiseguy Novelty Company in Walla Walla, Washington. Apparently, this company has been selling very dangerous Hypno-Rings. We now take you live, via satellite, to our reporter, Booger Stinkersquirt, er, I mean, Larry Zarrow, with the latest developments."

"Thanks, Chim-Chim," said Larry. "Reports have poured in from all across the country concerning children who have used the 3-D Hypno-Ring on their friends and family with disastrous results. But the most shocking revelation is the effect that the rings seem to have on *women*.

"Apparently, whenever the ring is used to hypnotize a woman, a mental blunder occurs, causing the woman to do the OPPOSITE of what she is being hypnotized to do.

"Doctors don't know why the ring causes women to have an OPPOSITE reaction, but they are very concerned. If you or someone you love has purchased a 3-D Hypno-Ring, throw it away at once. And whatever you do, PLEASE DON'T USE IT ON A WOMAN!"

79

CHAPTER 14³/4
WE NOW RETURN TO OUR REGULARLY SCHEDULED CHAPTER
(ALREADY IN PROGRESS...)

". . . and when we snap our fingers," George continued, "you will change our grades back to normal."

"Yeah," said Harold. "And you won't do anything crazy, like turn into *Wedgie Woman*."

"And you won't try to destroy Captain Underpants," said George, "or take over the world, either."

"Right!" said Harold. "You'll just change our grades, and that's it!"

George and Harold looked nervously at each other.

"Well," said George, "I think that covers everything."

"Yep," said Harold. "We shouldn't have any more problems from Ms. Ribble."

So the boys snapped their fingers.

SNAP!

81

CHAPTER 15
BAD HAIR NIGHT

That night, George and Harold camped out in George's tree house.

"I have to drive your mother to work early tomorrow morning," said George's dad. "So you boys are responsible for getting yourselves to school on time."

"OK, Pop," said George.

"We'll be there bright and early, Mr. Beard," said Harold.

It had been a tough day for George and
Harold, and now it was time to relax. George
rolled out the sleeping bags, while Harold
unpacked a box of chocolate donuts, four
cans of orange cream soda, and a big bowl of
Bar-B-Q potato chips. Believe it or not, there
was even a cool Japanese monster movie
playing on TV.

"You know," said George, "life doesn't get
any better than this!"

"Yep," said Harold. "But do you think the
Hypno-Ring actually worked on Ms. Ribble?
She looked a little weird when she came out
of her trance."

"Aaah, she was probably just sleepy," said
George. "Teachers have very stressful jobs,
you know."

"I wonder why?" said Harold.

83

After the movie, George and Harold
brushed the crumbs out of their sleeping
bags and got ready for bed.

"Let's sleep in our school clothes tonight,"
said George. "That way we won't have to
wake up early to get dressed."

"Good idea," said Harold.

So George turned out the light, and soon
the two boys were drifting off to sleep. After a
few minutes, Harold sat up quickly and
looked around.

"Hey!" he whispered. "What's that noise?"

"I didn't hear anything," said George.

84

They listened closely.

"Shhh!" said Harold. "There it is again!"

George heard it this time. He reached over and opened the tree house door a crack. All they could hear was the sound of crickets chirping in the night. George opened the door wider, and the boys peeked down.

85

"AAAUUGH!" roared an evil-looking woman dressed in tight purple vinyl and a mangy-looking fake-fur boa.

George and Harold screamed in horror!

The snarling woman climbed from the ladder into the tree house. George and Harold recognized her immediately in the moonlight.

86

"Ms. Ribble," George gasped. "What a lovely, uh, *outfit* you have on."

"Who's Ms. Ribble?" the angry lady growled. "My name is *Wedgie Woman*!!!"

George and Harold looked at each other and swallowed hard.

"I understand that you boys have information about Captain Underpants," said Wedgie Woman.

"What makes you say that?" asked Harold.

"I've read your comic books," said the evil villain. "You boys know his strengths, his weaknesses, and I'll bet you even know his SECRET IDENTITY!"

"No way!" said George. "Captain Underpants isn't real . . . He—he's just a cartoon!"

"We'll see about that," Wedgie Woman scoffed.

Wedgie Woman reached out and grasped George's and Harold's arms.

"What do we do now?" cried Harold.

"We can take 'er," said George. "It's not like she has super powers or anything!"

CHAPTER 16
WHO'S AFRAID OF THE BIG BAD BEEHIVE?

The struggle that followed may someday be remembered as the single most unlucky thing that ever happened in the history of the world.

First, George pulled his arm out of Wedgie Woman's grasp. Then Harold squirmed away, too. When Wedgie Woman lunged after them, George crouched down into a ball behind Wedgie Woman's feet. All it took was a simple nudge from Harold to send the ferocious female toppling over backward . . .

. . . right into the wall. KLUNK! The bookshelf above Wedgie Woman's head shook violently, causing a strange-looking juice carton to topple over. Suddenly, a stream of glowing green juice poured out of the carton, directly into the tightly woven beehive of hair atop Wedgie Woman's head.

"NOOO!" yelled Harold as he grabbed the juice carton. "This is the juice we got from that spaceship back in our third book!"

"You mean the one with the annoyingly long title?" asked George.

"Yeah!" said Harold. "This is Extra-Strength Super Power Juice! And a whole bunch of it got in her hair!"

"Don't worry," said George. "None of it got in her mouth. What's the worst thing that could happen? Her *hairstyle* would have super powers?"

"Well," said Harold, "I guess you're right. That *is* pretty stupid . . . even for one of *our* stories!"

"It's pretty funny, though," said George.

91

Suddenly, two coiled arms of twisting hair shot out of Wedgie Woman's head and grabbed George and Harold by the back of their underwear, yanking them high into the air.

"You know," said George, "this isn't as funny as I thought it would be."

CHAPTER 17
ALL TIED UP

Wedgie Woman brought George and Harold back to her house and tied the boys tightly to two chairs.

"Tell me the secret identity of Captain Underpants!" screamed Wedgie Woman.

"No way!" said George.

"Hmmmm," said Wedgie Woman. "You want to do this the hard way? *No problem!*"

Wedgie Woman's hair began uncoiling itself. Several twisted locks of hair stretched out into the living room and started taking apart the television, the computer, and a ThighMaster®.

Other tangled coils reached into the kitchen and began dismantling the dishwasher, the toaster oven, and a Ronco Food Dehydrator.

"What are you doing?" asked Harold.

"If you want to make robots," said Wedgie Woman, "you gotta break a few small appliances!"

MEANEST TEACHER OF THE YEAR AWARD

George and Harold watched impatiently while Wedgie Woman's hair assembled thousands of assorted screws, bolts, wires, gears, cathode tubes, and computer chips. Soon, two small robots began taking shape.

"I didn't know Ms. Ribble was smart enough to make robots," said Harold.

"Me, neither," said George. "I think some of that Extra-Strength Super Power Juice must have soaked into her *brain*!"

The next morning, Wedgie Woman completed her robots, which she named "Robo-George" and "The Harold 2000."

"You know," said Harold, "something about those robots seems a little *familiar*!"

"Yeah," said George. "They kinda look like us . . . only not as dashingly handsome."

Wedgie Woman opened the robots' chest plates and inserted a can of spray starch into each one. Then she sealed the chest plates, patted each robot on the head, and sent them both off to school. "Captain Underpants doesn't stand a chance now!" Wedgie Woman laughed.

"Wait a minute," said Harold. "How are those two robots going to stop Captain Underpants?"

"All they have to do is wait and listen," said Wedgie Woman. "And as soon as they hear the words 'Tra-La-Laaaaa!', *it'll all be over!*"

CHAPTER 18
ROBO-GEORGE AND
THE HAROLD 2000

"Uh, attention boys and girls," said Mr. Krupp
to the fourth graders. "Your teacher, Ms.
Ribble, didn't come to school today."

"Hooray!" shouted the children.

"*Settle down!*" Mr. Krupp shouted. "You're
still going to have all your classes!"

"Aww, *maaaan!*" moaned the children.

"But you're going to have a substitute
teacher," said Mr. Krupp.

"Hooray!" shouted the children.

"And it's going to be *me!*" said Mr. Krupp.

"Aww, *maaaan!*" moaned the children.

The whole day was pretty much like a normal day, except for one thing: Mr. Krupp couldn't understand why George and Harold were so well behaved.

They didn't make funny noises during science class, they didn't stick crayons up their noses during art class, and they didn't draw comic books during math class. In fact, they even walked past a sign without changing the letters around. Mr. Krupp was stunned.

"Alright, you two!" Mr. Krupp shouted. "I know you're up to something . . . You better stop being so good, or you're gonna be in *BIG TROUBLE*!"

But Robo-George and the Harold 2000 kept right on behaving. The only time they did something even remotely wrong was during recess. Everybody was playing kickball, and when it was the Harold 2000's turn to kick the ball, he kicked it pretty darn hard.

KA-BOINGGG!

101

The v
normal
couldn

The kickball tore right through the top of page 101 and out the other side as it sailed toward the outer regions of Earth's atmosphere. Soon it broke free of our planet's gravitational pull and began heading straight toward the planet Uranus.

"A-HA!" shouted Mr. Krupp, as he pulled out the official school rulebook and read Rule #411 out loud: *It is against the rules to kick school property into outer space!* You're in trouble now, bub!"

102

But the Harold 2000 ignored Mr. Krupp and began running around the bases.

"Hey! I'm talking to you, Hutchins!" Mr. Krupp shouted. He pointed at the Harold 2000 and snapped his fingers.

SNAP!

SNAP!

Big Book O' Rules

Suddenly, Mr. Krupp began to change. A silly-looking smile stretched across his face, and he stood before the fourth graders looking quite heroic. Quickly, he turned and ran back into the school.

104

CHAPTER 19
TRA-LA-LUUUNATICS

Several minutes later, Captain Underpants flew out of Mr. Krupp's office window. As the hero zipped across the sky, he let out a triumphant "Tra-La-Laaaaa!"

When Robo-George and the Harold 2000 heard the words "Tra-La-Laaaaa!", they immediately stopped playing kickball. Suddenly, their arms began to extend and their legs stretched toward the sky.

Strange secret compartments in their ever-growing torsos opened up, revealing giant rocket boosters and the latest in advanced aviation technology. Steel panels on their faces and bodies expanded wildly as their complex structures swelled to highly improbable proportions.

Suddenly, flames shot out of their retro-thrusters as their bodies rose into the air. In no time at all, two gigantic robots were flying in hot pursuit of the Amazing Captain Underpants.

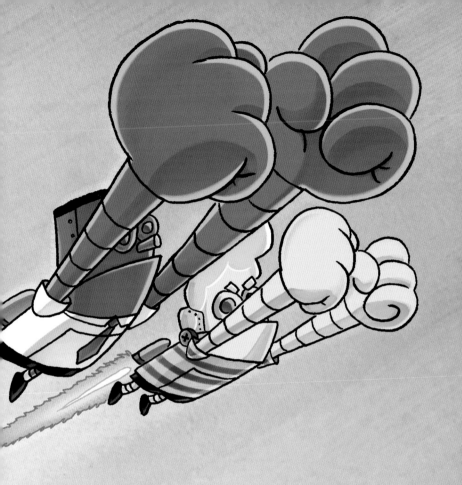

"George and Harold are in BIG trouble now," said Melvin Sneedly, as he read Rule #7,734 of Mr. Krupp's official school rulebook out loud: *"It is against the rules for students to transform into giant flying robots during afternoon recess!"*

The *real* George and Harold, however, had more on their minds at that moment than a few broken rules. They watched the action unfold on a big-screen television that Wedgie Woman's horrible hair had built by combining the spare parts of a fish tank and an electric toothbrush.

The colossal robots surrounded Captain Underpants, but surprisingly, the Waistband Warrior looked happy to see them.

"George! Harold!" said Captain Underpants. "My, how you boys have grown! And I didn't know you could fly. That's great! Now you can help me fight for Truth, Justice, and all that is Pre-Shrunk and Cottony!"

But the gigantic robots didn't respond.
Instead, they hovered close to Captain
Underpants as their steel chest plates opened
up. Suddenly, two extendable robotic arms
reached out and began showering Captain
Underpants with liquid spray starch.

"What—what are you doing?" cried
Captain Underpants. "That's *SPRAY STARCH*!
It's the only thing in the world that can take
away my super powers!!!"

The Waistband Warrior screamed in
horror as he began falling through the
sky. Robo-George quickly swooped down,
grabbed the helpless hero, and hung him
by his waistband on a tall pole high above
the city streets.

110

CHAPTER 20
YOU AXED FOR IT

"Hooray!" cried Wedgie Woman as she turned off her new TV. "My plan worked. Now it's time to take over the world!"

"But what about us?" asked Harold.

"Don't worry," said Wedgie Woman. "I've got a big surprise for you two." She took a heavy battle-axe and tied it up with a rope. Then she leaned the axe toward George and Harold and lit a candle under the rope.

"When the flame burns through the rope," said Wedgie Woman, "all your problems will be over. Get the point?"

"Not really," said George.

"Don't worry," laughed Wedgie Woman. "You will soon enough."

Wedgie Woman laughed a horrible laugh. Then she dashed out the door to take on the world!

George and Harold watched as the flame began burning through the rope. They cringed as the impending doom of the axe blade came closer and closer.

"Well," said George, "it looks like this is the end."

"Maybe not," said Harold. "Maybe the blade will fall and slice through our ropes and not harm us at all."

"I doubt it," said George. "That kind of thing only happens in really lame adventure stories."

112

Suddenly, the blade fell and sliced through the ropes, not harming George or Harold at all. The two boys looked at each other and decided it was best not to comment on the situation.

Thok

CHAPTER 21
THE WOOTHLESS WEVENGE OF THE WICKED WEDGIE WOMAN

Wedgie Woman headed to the center of town to meet up with Robo-George and the Harold 2000. "Well done, my precious robots," said Wedgie Woman affectionately.

"What's all this then?" said a policeman who had just arrived on the scene.

"Er—nothing, officer," said Wedgie Woman. "Just the beginning of my TOTAL WORLD DOMINATION!"

"Oh, OK," said the cop. "Hey, *wait a minute*!" But before the police officer could voice his objections, a twisted strand from Wedgie Woman's head shot out and grabbed the cop by the back of his underwear.

115

The colossal Harold 2000 lifted the
officer and hung him from a stop sign.

"Owie, *WOWIE*!" cried the cop.

Soon more police officers headed to
the scene, but they all met with the same
terrible fate as the first policeman.

Before long, every cop in the city
was hanging from a street sign.

"Call the National Guard!" screamed
the Chief of Police. "Call the Army —
call the Marines — call a *HAIRSTYLIST*!"

117

Soon, the armed forces arrived with a whole fleet of tanks and helicopters. But everybody was afraid to shoot. Wedgie Woman was just too quick.

The giant robots stomped around the city as Wedgie Woman barked out her commands. "Everybody on Earth must obey ME!" cried the Wicked Wedgie Woman. "If anybody refuses, they'll get the WEDGE! If anybody tries to stop me, it's WEDGIE TIME! Bow down to me . . . or *WELCOME TO WEDGIEVILLE*!"

Soon George and Harold arrived at the scene. They hid in some bushes and watched the terror unfold.

"We've got to rescue Captain Underpants," whispered George. "He's the only one who can save the world!"

"But how?" whispered Harold. "He's got no super powers left!"

"Sure he does!" said George. "Starch doesn't really take away super powers . . . he just *THINKS* it does. We've got to change his mind!"

"I sure hope we can!" said Harold.

CHAPTER 22
THEY CAN'T

George and Harold ran to the pole where the heartbroken hero was hanging.

"Hey, Captain Underpants," cried Harold. "You've got to come down from there and save the city!"

"C-Can't," whined the Waistband Warrior. "N-Need fabric softener!"

"No you *don't* need fabric softener!" said George sternly. "That was just a dumb joke in one of our comics!"

"But you don't understand," said Captain Underpants. "Starch is the enemy of underwear. Only fabric softener can save me!"

"*RATS!*" said Harold in frustration. "Hey, George, are there any stores around here?"

"Yeah," said George. "A new one just opened down on Oak Street."

"Then let's go buy some fabric softener," said Harold. "It'll be easier than trying to reason with the guy."

"How's that going to help?" asked George.

"It's all in his mind," Harold explained. "If he *believes* that fabric softener will save him, then it probably will. I think it's called 'the Placenta Effect.'"

So George and Harold ran to Oak Street. "What's the name of that store?" asked Harold.

"I can't remember," said George. "I think it's called 'Everything Except . . . umm —'"

EVERYTHING EXCEPT FABRIC SOFTENER
THE STORE FOR ALL YOUR NON-FABRIC SOFTENING NEEDS
OPEN 24 HOURS
SALE SALE

SLAP

SLAP

"Aww, *maaaan!*" said George.
"*We're doomed!*" cried Harold.
"Listen," said George, "we've got
to make another comic book!"
"Now?!!?" asked Harold.

122

"It's our only hope," said George. "The fate of the entire planet is in our hands!"

So the two boys bought some paper and a few pencils, and got down to work.

Twenty-two minutes later, George and Harold had created an all-new Captain Underpants adventure. They ran back to the pole where Captain Underpants was hanging and tossed their new comic up to him.

"This is no time to be reading comics," said Captain Underpants.

"Just read it, bub!" said Harold.

"Yeah," said George. "You might learn something!"

CHAPTER 23
THE ORIGIN OF CAPTAIN UNDERPANTS

THE TRUE **UNTOLD** STORY!

By George Beard
and
Harold Hutchins

THE ORIJIN OF CAPTAIN UNDERPANTS

the TRUE UNTOLD STORY BY G. BEard and H. Hutchins

A far time Ago in a Galaxy Long, Long Away...

...there WAS A Planet Called Underpantyworld.

Underpantyworld was A peaseful Planet where everybody wore only Underwear.

HA HA I can see your underwear.

Hey what are you doing under there?

Under where?

I can see yours to. Ha Ha Ha

Ha Ha You Said "Under wear"

Ha Ha

EveryBody Liked wearing Underwear so much that they never got into Fights and they dident have no wars either. It was CooL.

But one day all of that happyness ended uBRuptly.

(Bad guys)

WW

STARCH Ship Enterprize

The wedgie WARLORDS hAd ARived !!!

Hey Boss, Lets spray that planet with starch!

Ok, I hate Those guys!

VIEWER SCREEN

The good People of Underpantyworld got Ascared. So they RAN To There Leader, "Big Daddy Long Johns"

Help US, BiG Daddy Long Johns!

OK.

Don't worry. I have a majic Amyoulet that will protect us from starch!

Yipee!

But he Acksid-entelly dropped the majic Amyoulet.

oopsies.

It fell into the mouth of his newborn Son, "Little Baby Underpants."

GULP.

OH NO--- He Swallowed it! We're Are Doomed

Just then the Wedgie WARlords sprayed Starch on Underpantyworld.

WW

STARCH Ship ENTERPRIZE

SSSSSSSS

Big Daddy Long Johns and his Lovely wife "Princess Pantyhose" knew that there planet was a goner. So they desided to save there baby.

Burp.

So they stretched his underwear real far.

STRECH

Then they Let go And shot him Into Space.

weeeee

ZING

Be Good!

Don't Pick Your nose!

Little Baby Underpants SAiled Threw space as his home planet Crumbled behind him.

AW, MAN

BOOM

Soon Little BABY Underpants FELL To Earth.

BONK

WELCOME To EARTH

Little Baby got Adopded by some old guys.

my he's so CUTE LETS Adop him

O.K.

They named him "Captain" After there Faverite cereal.

Hi "Captain"

Hi

CAPT CRUN

BuT as the years wenT by, Captain Became very Sad. For some STRANGE reason, he never ever seemed To Fit in.

Why do I Feel so diferent?

Then one ~~day~~ night he had a weird dream.

ssss

He saw his old planet and his other parents.

Hi son

Hows it Going?

Son, You aren't like other people. You are a super hero guy.

Also, you have a majical Amyoulet inside you. It will protect you from the evils of starch!

All you half to do is say these words: "I SUMMON THE POWER OF UNDERPANTYWORLD." And you will overcome the powers of starch!

ok

So captain awoke up and Became a cool super hero guy...

And he never had to be Ascared of starch No more (even if wedgie womans Robots sprayed him with it) Because all he had to do was say "I SUMMON The POWER OF UNDERPANTYWORLD" And he would be Free!!!

WELL? WHAT ARE YOU WAITING FOR??? JUST SAY THE WORDS!!!

TREE HOUSE COMIX INC.

CHAPTER 24
THE PLACENTA EFFECT

"Wow," said Captain Underpants. "I didn't realize that I had the power within me all along to overcome the evils of starch."

"JUST SAY THE WORDS!" shouted George and Harold.

"OK," said Captain Underpants. "But I think it's a great metaphor for —"

"JUST SAY THE WORDS!" yelled George and Harold.

"*Alright!*" said Captain Underpants. "But all I'm saying is that—"

"*JUST SAY THE WORDS!*" screamed George and Harold.

"You know," said Captain Underpants, "you kids have *NO* feel for dramatic tension!" Then he cleared his throat and spoke in a powerful voice. "I SUMMON THE POWER OF UNDERPANTYWORLD!" Suddenly, Captain Underpants rose triumphantly into the air. He was free at last!

When the gigantic robots saw that Captain Underpants had escaped, the Harold 2000 launched its rocket arms at our hero.

Captain Underpants grabbed the giant robo-arms and swung them around toward his foes.

"These might come in handy," said the Waistband Warrior.

CHAPTER 25
THE INCREDIBLY GRAPHIC VIOLENCE CHAPTER (IN FLIP-O-RAMA™)

WARNING:

The following chapter contains scenes that are so violent and naughty, you aren't allowed to view them.

We're not kidding.

DO NOT READ THE FOLLOWING CHAPTER!

Don't even look at it. Just skip ahead to page 156, and don't ask any questions.

P.S. Don't breathe on it, either.

137

INTRODUCING FLIP.

Hey, what are you doing here? You're not supposed to be looking at this chapter — it's too violent and naughty!

Now bend over and give yourself eleven spankings and a time-out before proceeding to the next page. Maybe then you'll learn to follow instructions!

PILKEY® BRAND

⌐RAMA

HERE'S HOW IT WORKS!

STEP 1

First, give yourself eleven spankings and one time-out. Then, place your *left* hand inside the dotted lines marked "LEFT HAND HERE." Hold the book open *flat*.

STEP 2

Grasp the *right-hand* page with your right thumb and index finger (inside the dotted lines marked "RIGHT THUMB HERE").

STEP 3

Now *quickly* flip the right-hand page back and forth until the picture appears to be *animated*.

(For extra fun, try adding your own sound-effects!)

FLIP-O-RAMA 1

(pages 141 and 143)

Remember, flip *only* page 141.
While you are flipping, be sure you
can see the picture on page 141
and the one on page 143.
If you flip quickly, the two
pictures will start to look like
<u>one</u> *animated* picture.

Don't forget to
add your own sound-effects!

LEFT HAND HERE

ROUGHIN' UP
ROBO-GEORGE

141

RIGHT
THUMB
HERE

RIGHT
INDEX
FINGER
HERE

ROUGHIN' UP ROBO-GEORGE

FLIP-O-RAMA 2

(pages 145 and 147)

Remember, flip *only* page 145.
While you are flipping, be sure you
can see the picture on page 145
and the one on page 147.
If you flip quickly, the two
pictures will start to look like
<u>one</u> *animated* picture.

Don't forget to
add your own sound-effects!

LEFT HAND HERE

HORRIBLY HURTIN' THE HAROLD 2000

RIGHT THUMB HERE

RIGHT
INDEX
FINGER
HERE

146

HORRIBLY HURTIN' THE HAROLD 2000

FLIP-O-RAMA 3

(pages 149 and 151)

Remember, flip *only* page 149.
While you are flipping, be sure you
can see the picture on page 149
and the one on page 151.
If you flip quickly, the two
pictures will start to look like
<u>one</u> *animated* picture.

Don't forget to
add your own sound-effects!

LEFT HAND HERE

LET'S PUT OUR
HEADS TOGETHER!

149

RIGHT
THUMB
HERE

RIGHT
INDEX
FINGER
HERE

150

LET'S PUT OUR
HEADS TOGETHER!

FLIP-O-RAMA 4

(pages 153 and 155)

Remember, flip *only* page 153.
While you are flipping, be sure you
can see the picture on page 153
and the one on page 155.
If you flip quickly, the two
pictures will start to look like
<u>one</u> *animated* picture.

Don't forget to
add your own sound-effects!

LEFT HAND HERE

THE SUPER-SMASHY CYBER SLAM

153

RIGHT THUMB HERE

RIGHT
INDEX
FINGER
HERE

154

THE SUPER-SMASHY CYBER SLAM

156

CHAPTER 26
REVERSE PSYCHOLOGY 2

The giant robots were defeated, but the battle was not over yet. Harold ran back to their tree house to grab the 3-D Hypno-Ring, while George ran back to Everything Except Fabric Softener for some more supplies.

157

Soon George returned to the center of town carrying a big cardboard box filled with spray cans.

"What are you doing with that?" asked Harold, who had just arrived with the 3-D Hypno-Ring.

"I'm taking this *Extra-Strength Spray Starch* someplace where Wedgie Woman won't be able to find it!" George shouted rather loudly.

"Extra-Strength Spray Starch?" cried the Wicked Wedgie Woman. "That's just what I need!" Her winding hair lashed out at George, stopping him dead in his tracks. Then nine twisting braids each grabbed a can from the box and began spraying them at Captain Underpants.

159

A huge cloud of mist filled the air, covering everything in sight, and making these two pages incredibly easy to draw.

When the cloud finally lifted, all of Wedgie Woman's hair was gone. In fact, all of EVERYBODY'S hair was gone.

"See?" George explained. "There was no spray starch in this box. This box was just a cleverly disguised carton of hair remover. I used *reverse psychology* on her."

"Aaugh!" screamed Harold, as he clutched his bald head. "My mom's gonna lay hard-boiled eggs when she sees me!"

"Relax," said George. "Our hair will grow back!"

"That's easy for you to say," said Harold. "Your hair was only half an inch long!"

CHAPTER 27
REVERSE REVERSE
PSYCHOLOGY

"Well, Wedgie Woman," said Captain Underpants. "It's off to jail with you!"

"Wait a second," said Harold. "We'll take care of Wedgie Woman. You go back to the school, put some clothes on, then wash your face."

"Yeah, bub," said George. "Use plenty of water! We've got work to do."

"OK," said Captain Underpants.

So Captain Underpants did as he was told, and in no time at all he was back to his Kruppy old self. It was now time to transform Wedgie Woman back to her old self, too . . . *with some slight modifications*.

"OK," said Harold, "remember when we hypnotized Ms. Ribble, and she did the opposite of everything we wanted her to do?"

"Yeah," said George.

"Well, if we want to set things right," Harold continued, "we've got to hypnotize her into doing the *opposite* of the opposite of what we want."

"I'm way ahead of you," said George.

165

So the two boys once again hypnotized their teacher. Only this time, they used reverse *reverse* psychology on her.

"From now on," said George, "you will ALWAYS be known as Wedgie Woman."

"You WILL keep all your super powers, too," said Harold.

"You WILL NOT go back to teaching fourth grade," said George.

"You WILL remember everything that happened in the last two weeks," said Harold.

"You WILL NOT change our grades back to normal," said George.

"You WILL NOT become the nicest teacher in the history of Jerome Horwitz Elementary School," said Harold.

"And you WILL NOT bake fresh chocolate chip cookies for our class every day," said George.

"*George!*" said Harold sternly. "Stop goofing around!"

"I can't help it," said George. "You should never hypnotize anybody when you're hungry!"

"OK, OK," said Harold. "Let's just snap our fingers and PRAY that this works."

SNAP!

CHAPTER 28
TO MAKE A LONG STORY SHORT

It did.

CHAPTER 29
BETTER LIVING
THROUGH HYPNOSIS

The next day, Ms. Ribble entered the classroom looking a whole lot friendlier than usual.

"Boys and girls," said Ms. Ribble, "I have some good news for you."

"Hooray!" cried the children.

"It's time for English class," said Ms. Ribble.

"Aww, *maaaan*," moaned the children.

"Today," said Ms. Ribble, "I've asked George and Harold to lead the class."

"Hooray!" cried the children.

"They're going to teach us about creative writing . . ." said Ms. Ribble.

"Aww, *maaaan*," moaned the children.

". . . by showing us how to make our own comic books!" said Ms. Ribble.

"Hooray!" cried the children.

"While they're doing that," said Ms. Ribble, "I'm going to pass out something for you all to work on . . ."

"Aww, *maaaan*," moaned the children.

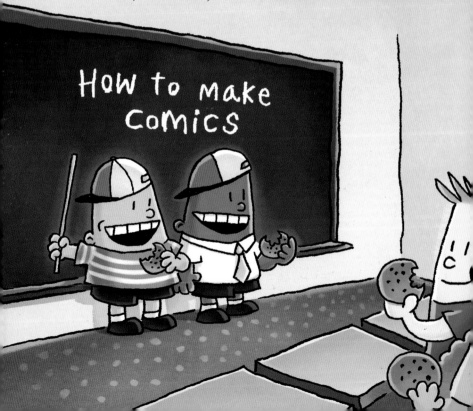

". . . Homemade chocolate chip cookies!" said Ms. Ribble.

"Hooray!" cried the children.

"This is awesome," said Harold, "but do you think it was right for us to change her personality like we did?"

"Sure, why not?" said George. "She's happier. She'll probably live longer!"

"You're right," said Harold. "I guess hypnosis is a pretty cool thing sometimes."

Then again (as we all know) sometimes it isn't.

Were these Cookies hard to make?

No, dear. They were A **SNAP!**

WALLY'S WIG WORLD

SNAP

"OH, NO!" screamed Harold.
"Here we go again!" screamed George.

TRA·LA·

ZAAAA!

ABOUT THE AUTHOR-ILLUSTRATOR

When Dav Pilkey was a kid, he was diagnosed with ADHD and dyslexia. Dav was so disruptive in class that his teachers made him sit out in the hallway every day. Luckily, Dav loved to draw and make up stories. He spent his time in the hallway creating his own original comic books — the very first adventures of Dog Man and Captain Underpants.

In college, Dav met a teacher who encouraged him to illustrate and write. He won a national competition in 1986 and the prize was the publication of his first book, WORLD WAR WON. He made many other books before being awarded the 1998 California Young Reader Medal for DOG BREATH, which was published in 1994, and in 1997 he won the Caldecott Honor for THE PAPERBOY.

THE ADVENTURES OF SUPER DIAPER BABY, published in 2002, was the first complete graphic novel spin-off from the Captain Underpants series and appeared at #6 on the USA Today bestseller list for all books, both adult and children's, and was also a New York Times bestseller. It was followed by THE ADVENTURES OF OOK AND GLUK: KUNG FU CAVEMEN FROM THE FUTURE and SUPER DIAPER BABY 2: THE INVASION OF THE POTTY SNATCHERS, both USA Today bestsellers. The unconventional style of these graphic novels is intended to encourage uninhibited creativity in kids.

His stories are semi-autobiographical and explore universal themes that celebrate friendship, tolerance, and the triumph of the good-hearted.

Dav loves to kayak in the Pacific Northwest with his wife.